MIA MAYHEM

#1

IS A SUPERHERO!

BY **KARA WEST**   ILLUSTRATED BY **LEEZA HERNANDEZ**

LITTLE SIMON

New York   London   Toronto   Sydney   New Delhi

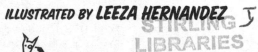

LITTLE SIMON
An imprint of Simon & Schuster Children's Publishing Division
1230 Avenue of the Americas, New York, New York 10020
First Little Simon paperback edition December 2018
Copyright © 2018 by Simon & Schuster, Inc.
Also available in a Little Simon hardcover edition
All rights reserved, including the right of reproduction in whole or in part in any form.
LITTLE SIMON is a registered trademark of Simon & Schuster, Inc., and associated colophon is a trademark of Simon & Schuster, Inc.
For information about special discounts for bulk purchases, please contact Simon & Schuster Special Sales at 1-866-506-1949 or business@simonandschuster.com.
The Simon & Schuster Speakers Bureau can bring authors to your live event. For more information or to book an event contact the Simon & Schuster Speakers Bureau at 1-866-248-3049 or visit our website at www.simonspeakers.com.
Designed by Laura Roode
Manufactured in the United States of America 1218 MTN
2 4 6 8 10 9 7 5 3
Library of Congress Cataloging-in-Publication Data
Names: West, Kara, author. | Hernandez, Leeza, illustrator.
Title: Mia Mayhem is a superhero! / by Kara West ; illustrated by Leeza Hernandez.
Description: First Little Simon paperback edition. | New York : Little Simon, 2018. | Series: Mia Mayhem ; 1 | Summary: Eight-year-old Mia Macarooney is delighted to learn she is from a family of superheroes, but her acceptance into the Program for In Training Superheroes requires she take a placement exam.
Identifiers: LCCN 2018033373 | ISBN 9781534432697 (paperback) ISBN 9781534432703 (hc) | ISBN 9781534432710 (eBook)
Subjects: | CYAC: Superheroes—Fiction. | Examinations—Fiction. | African Americans—Fiction. | BISAC: JUVENILE FICTION / Action & Adventure / General. | JUVENILE FICTION / Readers / Chapter Books.
Classification: LCC PZ7.1.W43684 Mi 2018 | DDC [E]—dc23
LC record available at https://lccn.loc.gov/2018033373

CONTENTS

THE UNEXPECTED LETTER

Okay, I know this doesn't look good. It definitely seems like a tornado just blew through my house. I spilled a whole bag of flour, broke a window, ran through the screen door, was licked by a bunch of dogs, and even got my shoe stuck in a tree.

But I have an excuse. Really, I do.

It's been a *super*-exciting day.

Seriously *super.* Why?

Well, hold on to your socks. . . .

Here's the deal:

You ready?

I. Mia Macarooney. Am.

A. Superhero!

For. *Real.* Yours truly has superpowers!

And believe it or not, I *just* found out myself. In fact, my life was completely ordinary . . . until this afternoon.

I had a normal, uneventful day at school, and my best friend, Eddie, and I walked home, just like every other single day ever. At my driveway, I checked the mailbox like I always did. Except today, there was a tattered letter covered in stamps . . . addressed to me!

3

It said:

DEAR MISS MIA MACAROONEY,

CONGRATULATIONS! WE'RE VERY PLEASED
TO INFORM YOU OF YOUR ACCEPTANCE
TO THE PROGRAM FOR IN TRAINING
SUPERHEROES (THE PITS). I LOOK
FORWARD TO MEETING YOU AT YOUR
FIRST SUPERHERO-TRAINING SESSION!

BEST WISHES,

Dr. Sue Perb

HEADMISTRESS

Uhh . . . *the program for in training what?* This couldn't be real.

I wasn't *super*. How could I be? I don't have superpowers! I'd definitely know if I did, right? Plus, I have a bit of a reputation for causing chaos and mayhem wherever I go.

I never mean to . . . but the truth is, I'm a total disaster-machine! Like one time I kicked a soccer ball that broke a steel goalpost in half. Another time, I flooded the hallways after using the water fountain.

So, you see what I mean? This couldn't be real.

I flipped over the letter to see if it said "GOTCHA!" on the back.

Nope. Nothing.

So I ran inside and triple-checked.

"You read that right. It's true, honey!" my mom exclaimed when I showed her the letter. "We've been waiting *forever*. We went to the PITS too!"

I looked up at her in total shock.

"This letter sure traveled a long way. We're thrilled for you, honey! You won't be *too* far behind," she said.

"Behind?" I asked.

"Well, you see, most kids start their training in kindergarten," Dad said.

I grabbed the piece of paper and read it again.

"No way! My letter is three years late?" I exclaimed.

"Don't worry, honey. You'll catch up as fast as lightning!" my dad said with a wink.

So just like that, I got the biggest, most unbelievable, best news ever! Can you believe it? All this time I thought I was a super-klutz . . . but turns out, I'm just *super*! *And* I always *have* been!

CHAPTER
2

My
SUPERFAMILY

"You might want to sit down for this," Mom said with a huge grin on her face.

I nervously backed into a chair as my cat, Chaos, jumped onto my lap.

"We're so happy we can finally tell you the Macarooney super-secret," Mom began slowly. "We're a family of superheroes!"

My jaw dropped to the floor.

"No way! So you're not really a flight attendant?" I asked.

"Of course I am!" she said, "But truth is, I can fly without a plane."

Okay, hold on. Did you just hear that?

This day has officially gone from really normal to really cool *super*fast.

"Wait a minute! Then are you really a veterinarian?" I asked my dad.

"Sure am! And I can talk to animals, too," he said. "Here, let me show you."

My dad looked straight into Chaos's eyes and started *meowing* . . . just like her!

MEOW, ME ME, MEOW!

WHEEEEE!

And believe it or not, my cat stood up and did a triple backflip onto the ground!

"Atta girl!" my dad said as they fist-bumped each other.

I sat back in shock, trying to take it all in. I couldn't believe it. I still had *so* many questions. But here's what I just learned: My cat is *way* smarter than I thought, my parents are real *superheroes* . . . and SO. AM. I!

"This is AWESOME!" I finally yelled out.

"Oh, Mia. We're thrilled for you!" my mom exclaimed. "We have to celebrate!"

"I know we already made cookies, but this news calls for more dessert!" my dad said.

I nodded excitedly. My dad always had good ideas.

POOF!

Well, it *was* a good idea . . . until I plopped the bag of flour down on the counter. *POOF!*

Flour got all over my face and even up my nose! Then Chaos started to run in circles, making the mess EVEN BIGGER!

I tried *really* hard to ignore the tickle in my nose, which turned out to be another not-so-good idea . . . because I sneezed so loudly that the big kitchen window CRACKED!

I swear I didn't mean to make things worse.

But it was too late. The noise made Chaos run off in an absolute frenzy.

I quickly wiped my eyes and ran after her. But as I rounded the corner, I tripped and fell . . . and my sneaky cat ran off with my shoe!

So obviously, I chased after her as fast as I could.

The only problem is, my top speed is a little *too* fast, even in crazy cat emergencies like this, because I tore through the screen door . . . and now there's a giant hole in it as big as me!

CHAPTER 3

Stuck Up
A Tree

Whoops!

I swear I didn't mean to burst through the door.

But believe it or not, I'm pretty used to craziness like this. Me and my cat both are! That's why I named her Chaos. She just *loves* messes!

And unfortunately for me, she's also *really good* at running away.

"Chaos! Where are you?" I hollered
as I looked around my backyard.

I kept yelling until I heard a soft cry.
From all the way up a tree!

"Chaos! What are you doing up
there?" I exclaimed. I could tell by the
look in her eyes that she couldn't get
down. I started pacing back and forth
nervously.

You see, I know I can climb up . . . because I *am* pretty strong. The only problem is, I absolutely hate heights. So I stood still, thinking *really hard* about what to do, when all of a sudden, there was a loud noise.

Oh no! Did I somehow break the fence just by *thinking*?

I know it sounds crazy. But now that I'm a SUPERHERO, anything can happen, right?

I held my breath, expecting the fence to break. But instead, a pack of dogs bounded over, circled me, and started barking.

I froze with my hands over my ears until I heard someone call my name.

"Don't worry, Mia! They won't hurt you," my dad exclaimed. "They heard Chaos's cry and came over to warn me!"

Then my dad ran over and started *barking at* the dogs. Every single one of them immediately calmed down.

"Ah, that's better," Dad said with a grin.

ARF!

ARF!

YIP!

YIP!

"And don't worry, Chaos!" Mom exclaimed. "I'll be right there!"

My mom then flew into the air as my jaw dropped to the ground.

Whoa. Did you just see that? MY MOM CAN *REALLY* FLY!

When she landed with Chaos safely in her arms, I ran over and gave them a huge hug.

I can't believe my parents just saved the day!

CHAPTER 4

LIVING IN A NORMAL WORLD

"Wow, I'm sorry. I really didn't mean to . . . ," I began as we walked back into the house.

"It's okay, Mia. I'm just glad you and Chaos are safe," my mom replied.

"And luckily, we have some extra help!" Dad said, pointing to the dogs.

Wait, hold on. Did I just *not* get into trouble?

That's not what
I was expecting . . .
but I could definitely
get used to
this!

My dad
then gave each
dog a job. They immediately started
cleaning food, books, and cushions off
the ground.

"This is amazing!" I cried.
"With your powers, this mess
will be gone in a flash!"
"Oh, Mia, you'll
learn all kinds of

super-skills at the PITS," Mom said
with a smile. "But it's important to
know that with great power comes
great responsibility."

"Like protecting you and saving
Chaos, for example," Dad continued.
"That's what superheroes do!"

"But since we live in a normal world, we also have to protect ourselves," Mom explained,  "by maintaining our secret identities."

"That's why we hold everyday jobs, why you will still go to your regular school, and why we do *most* things the old-fashioned way . . . with a few special exceptions," Dad added with a wink.

Then he turned to the hole in the screen door and shot lasers *out of his hands*! And just like that it was repaired.

"Wow. That's awesome!" I exclaimed as I grabbed a regular old broom.

Luckily, even without any special help, we finished cleaning in no time. Then we made brownies by hand, just like we had planned.

But as I was washing up, I realized there was just one tiny problem.

"Mom, how am I supposed to keep this super-secret from everyone?" I asked.

"Oh, don't worry. You can't possibly keep it a secret from *everyone*," Mom replied. "Even superheroes need people they can trust."

"Oh thank goodness!" I exclaimed.

This was great news . . . because I am absolutely *terrible* at keeping secrets. Especially from Eddie.

So as soon as the oven beeped, I grabbed some brownies, shoved the acceptance letter into my pocket, and ran out the door.

PURR!

PURR!

CHAPTER 5

SPILLING THE BEANS

"These brownies look delicious, Mia!" Eddie's mom exclaimed when she opened the door.

"Oh yes! They're yummy, Mrs. Stein!" I replied as I gave her one.

Then I ran to Eddie's room and burst open the door. I may have pushed a little *too* hard though because a gust of wind blew through the room!

I lifted my hand to make it stop. And thankfully, it worked! The wind calmed down. The only problem was, *everything else* froze too!

Oh man. I have no idea what I just did. But see that kid over there? The one who looks totally surprised? His name is Edison Stein, or Eddie for short, and he's my best friend.

He's *super*smart. And he always has my back. Even when I cause mayhem. In fact, remember how I broke the goalpost? Well, Eddie was the goalie. And he told our coach that the post was already broken . . . and our coach believed it!

So I'm hoping Eddie won't be *too* mad about this. It looks like he's busy working on something *super*-important.

All I need to do is figure out how to unfreeze him.

"Umm . . .

"melt!"

I commanded.

Nothing.

"Undo!"

Nope.

"Simon says?"

I tried.

After a dozen commands, I gave up and reached my hand out in front of me.

And that actually worked!

"Uh, Mia?" Eddie called out. "Is that you?"

"Sorry! I got a little *too* excited," I replied.

"To bring me brownies?" he asked doubtfully as he grabbed one.

"Oh yeah, these brownies are so good," I replied as I took a deep breath. "But I've got something to tell you . . . and you have to *promise* you won't tell a soul."

So we did our secret handshake.

"Okay. This is crazy, but . . . I just found out that I'm not a super-klutz. I'm actually *super!*"

"Of course you are. You're great!" Eddie replied.

"No, like for real! I just found out I have . . . superpowers!"

He took a bite of his brownie and looked at me, clearly confused.

"Here, I have proof," I continued, pulling out the letter.

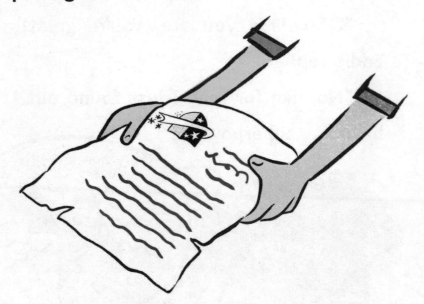

I filled him in on the mess that I made at my house, and then I waited patiently.

He flipped over the paper just like I had and read it again.

Still nothing. So I waited some more.

Then, after what felt like *forever*, he looked up at me with the biggest smile I've ever seen.

WELCOME TO THE PITS!

The next day, after the longest English class ever, my parents came to pick me up early. We were going to the PITS together for the first time . . . and I couldn't wait!

When we finally left, I expected to see a jet. Or a hovercraft. Or even a submarine! Because after all, we were going top secret superhero training academy, so it would only make sense to arrive in style, right?

So obviously, I couldn't believe it when we simply walked to an empty, abandoned warehouse . . . that was right next to my school!

"Umm . . . is the jet inside here?" I asked.

"The *what*?" my mom asked with a laugh. "No, honey. We're here!"

Wait. This must be a mistake. Are you seeing what I'm seeing?

This is an empty warehouse. This can't possibly be it!

There's even a crooked DO NOT ENTER sign dangling on the side.

I was about to tell her that we were *definitely* in the wrong place, when she reached out and straightened the sign.

Then guess what happened?

The concrete bricks *shifted* around . . . until a hidden screen popped up!

My parents knew exactly what to do. My mom and dad stood still. Then they opened their eyes wide as a red light carefully scanned their faces.

When the light turned green, a
secret entrance appeared . . . out of
nowhere!

A tall, elegant woman in a sleek,
black skintight suit was waiting for us
as soon as we walked in.

"Ah, it's so great to see you!" she said as she gave my parents a hug.

"Oh wow, and you must be Mia!" she exclaimed happily. "Welcome to the PITS! My name is Dr. Sue Perb."

When we arrived at the main lobby, I couldn't believe my eyes! From the outside this building looked like a boring, old warehouse. But on the inside, there were floor-to-ceiling windows and huge forty-foot-tall screens everywhere!

"Welcome to the Compass!" Dr. Perb exclaimed. "If you ever get lost, all you need to do is come back to the heart of the PITS."

I looked around in awe as we stood in the middle of a gigantic compass that was in the marble floor.

The crazy thing is, this wasn't even the coolest part!

63

Because there were actual real-life *superheroes* everywhere!

Dr. Perb must have seen my mouth hanging open because she turned to me and said, "It's a lot to take in, isn't it? We have the best superheroes teaching here. You're in good hands, Mia."

Wait. Did you hear that? That man with the winged suit is going to be my teacher!

And just when I thought things couldn't get *any* cooler, she led us into the fanciest headmistress's office EVER.

"First, we need to scan and secure your identity," Dr. Sue Perb said as she offered us seats. "So that you can enter the building!"

She typed away on her computer as a drone camera scanned my entire body.

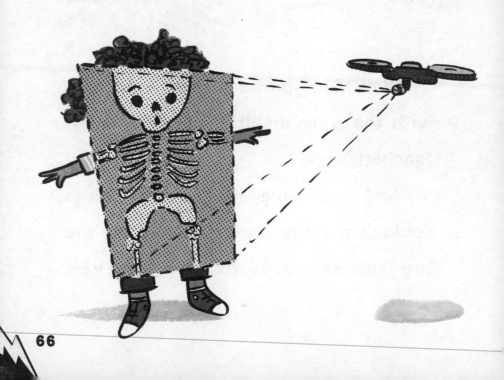

"You are now in the PITS Superhero Database!" she exclaimed minutes later. "You will get a full tour tomorrow, but I called you in before any students arrive because today is the first and last day you will come as Mia Macarooney.

Starting tomorrow, you are to come in your supersuit. You'll also be registered into our database under your very own superhero name! It's our top priority to protect your secret identity."

"But . . . I don't have a supersuit *or* a name!" I replied.

"Don't worry. We're going to take care of the supersuit," she said. "But your superhero name is up to you. You'll know exactly when you find it . . . but until then, simply going as 'Mia' is just fine."

Then she pulled a green leaf on her desk plant, and she spoke into it.

"Professor Stu Pendus, please come in."

A wall panel opened up, and a man burst out, shimmering in green.

"Mia, meet Professor Stu Pendus! He's the mastermind behind everyone's supersuit . . . including yours!"

Professor Stu Pendus led me into a huge room stocked with colorful fabrics, took my measurements, and started pulling things off the shelf.

A lot of them were *super*crazy.

And weird.

And totally
not me.

Until finally, we found it:

the perfect suit.

THE TOUR

At school the next day, the morning passed by *incredibly* slowly. I was so nervous that I couldn't sit still! But can you blame me? Today was my first day at the PITS, and I couldn't wait to meet other superheroes just like me!

I tapped my pencil on my desk as I watched the clock. When the bell rang, I jumped up as Eddie came over.

It was going to be weird not going home together, but I promised to tell him all about it.

Then I rushed into the bathroom to change . . . into my very own suit! But I'll definitely have to work on the quick-superhero-change thing . . . because before I knew it, I was running late!

Once I
arrived at
the warehouse,
I adjusted the
DO NOT ENTER
sign.

But nothing happened.

So I twirled it.
Pulled it.
Pushed it.
Still nothing.

I stood there totally confused till someone tapped me on the shoulder.

"It only works at a specific angle," a boy wearing a blazing red cape explained.

He tilted the sign and the screen appeared. I watched him as he scanned his face.

Then it was my turn. I did exactly as he did . . . and thankfully, it worked!

Dr. Sue Perb was waiting for me inside. "Ah, you two have already met!" she exclaimed. "Penn Powers, could you please show Mia around before her placement exam? You'll probably be in

some of the same classes. Today is her very first day."

"What? There's an exam?" I cried.

"Don't freak out. It's not a big deal. You can't study for it," Penn Powers replied rather coolly.

"He's right, Mia. There's nothing to worry about! Please enjoy your tour!"

Dr. Sue Perb exclaimed. I thanked her and then ran to catch up with Penn, who had already walked away.

Luckily, the nerves about the exam went away as we passed by classrooms for flying, strength training, super-speed, and my dad's special power . . . talking to animals.

"The building has five identical floors with hallways that all lead back to the Compass. Each wing of the PITS is dedicated to a specific superfield of study," Penn explained. "Beginner-level classes are on the first floor, and grand-master studies are at the top."

I listened very carefully, trying to take it all in.

"Wow, those kids are really flying!" I exclaimed as I peeked in to one of the rooms.

"Actually, they're learning how to jump. It's the most basic skill of flying," Penn replied matter-of-factly.

"When will I learn to do that?" I asked excitedly.

"Well, obviously, you'll find out after your exam. Until then, just come with me—I'm late for flying class!"

CHAPTER
8

PROFESSOR WINGUM'S FLYING CLASS

"What's on the third floor?" I asked as we rushed into a glass elevator.

"All advanced courses," he replied. "Most kids our age are on the second floor, in junior-level classes . . . but I'm a *super*-flier!"

Wow!

Did you hear that?

He must be really talented.

Okay, I'll be honest. Up until right now, I felt good about being a newbie superhero. After all, there's something that feels *super*-right about being with other kids . . . just like me! But now, I'm starting to feel pretty out of place.

When the elevator doors opened, I gasped for the hundredth time.

We were standing in front of the coolest obstacle course EVER! There was an awesome rock-climbing wall, a moving jungle gym, tightropes, and even floating monkey bars!

And guess what?

The same man in the winged suit from yesterday came flying toward us.

WHOOSH!

87

"Hello! You must be Mia. Dr. Suc Perb told me that Penn was taking you around," he said warmly. "My name is Professor Wingum."

As he landed to shake my hand, Penn flew off to join the rest of the kids.

I watched in awe as Penn dove through hoops, spun around poles, and glided above the water.

"Not bad, eh?" Professor Wingum asked proudly. "Penn is a natural."

I nodded my head in disbelief.

"I know you're taking your placement exam after this, but would you like to hop on the ropes?" Professor Wingum asked. "It'll help you get used to heights."

Now, watching Penn fly around must have made me feel *super*brave . . . because I surprisingly said yes.

I jumped onto the rope as Dr. Wingum spotted me from behind. And at first, going up was a piece of cake!

But I should have never looked down. Why?

Well, do you see that? Look at how high I am!

Worst. Idea. Ever.

Thankfully, though, it reminded me of the time I got stuck at the top of a Ferris wheel.

And I remembered what had calmed me down before.

Inhale.

Exhale.

Inhale.

Exhale.

In—

Are you wondering what that sound was?

Oh, don't worry. It's just the sound of . . . THE ROPE BREAKING!

I yelled out at the top of my lungs as I frantically swung back and forth. I hoped my loud shrieking would get someone's attention, but it was no use.

I was about to fall twenty feet . . . and
NO ONE COULD HEAR ME!

I shut my eyes and braced myself
for the worst. A horrible, nauseating
feeling in my stomach grew bigger and
bigger . . . until suddenly, like magic, it
disappeared!

Someone had come to the rescue!

I relaxed as we flew around in a circle. I was even enjoying the ride . . . until I opened my eyes.

I couldn't believe I was being carried to safety by . . . Penn Powers!

How embarrassing!

And unfortunately, things got even more awkward. Because when we landed, my legs totally gave out and Penn helped me up . . . *again*!

Then he proudly took a bow as everyone burst into applause.

THE WEIRDEST TEST EVER

Ugh. Are you kidding me?

No one told me these ropes were part of the exam!

I'm stuck here again. And there's no way I'm moving. Not even one inch.

I seriously can't believe I have to do this *again* after what I just went through in Professor Wingum's class.

This superhero business is no joke.

And it doesn't help that being stuck here is just as embarrassing as before . . . but embarrassing or not, I don't think flying is my thing.

So obviously, I did the same thing I did earlier: yell for mercy!

This time, Professor Dina Myte, Dr. Sue Perb's second in command, got me down . . . instead of Penn.

Being saved wasn't fun, but I hoped I'd

have better luck at talking to animals because after all . . . I had a cat!

Unfortunately, this wasn't the case. Because I somehow managed to offend a dog, confuse a bird, and put a newt to sleep!

zZZ Z

Now, before I go on, let me just say that yes, I was disappointed to know that I was not very good at *either* of my parents' skills.

But if my mom and dad have something special, I must have one too, right?

Well, I wish I could tell you that I found it. But . . . I didn't. And things just got weirder. Because during the strength-training portion, I had to lift an elephant *and* a car!

Then for superspeed, I fumbled my way through an obstacle course with a million hurdles!

After that, I had to try to make four pencils float in midair, freeze and unfreeze water droplets, and even try to shoot lasers out of my eyes!

Can you guess how it all went?

Yep, that's right. Not well. At all.

By the end of the last skill test, I was pooped.

And believe it or not, that wasn't even all of it!

"It's time for the written portion now!" Professor Myte exclaimed as she handed me a stack of papers.

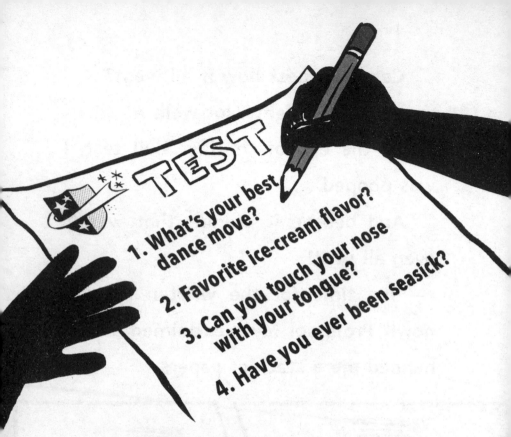

TEST

1. What's your best dance move?
2. Favorite ice-cream flavor?
3. Can you touch your nose with your tongue?
4. Have you ever been seasick?

The papers had a list with the most random questions.

After I wrote in my final answer, the longest day ever continued to drag on.

MAYHEM ARRIVES!

"How was your first day?" Dr. Sue Perb asked as I nervously walked into her office.

I looked down at my feet. Was I supposed to tell her how embarrassing and disastrous it was? Did she know that I got stuck on the ropes *twice* and was even saved by Penn Powers?

In the end I told her the truth.

"This place is *super*cool . . . but to be honest I'm not sure I'm cut out for this," I mumbled, trying not to cry.

"Oh, Mia. Every superhero is born with special powers, but becoming a *real* superhero takes work," she said warmly. "Believe it or not, superheroes aren't made overnight."

Then she handed me a piece of paper.

"Congratulations!" she exclaimed. "You're at the junior level for everything . . . . except flying and foreign languages. You'll be in beginner-level classes for those." She gave me a pat on the back as I looked at her in shock.

I grabbed the paper and looked closely.

How was this possible? I was so sure I'd failed!

"Is this for real?" I asked.

"Of course it is!" Dr. Sue Perb exclaimed. "Our exam is completely foolproof. Every training schedule is tailored to each student."

Then she reached out from under her desk and handed me my favorite ice cream!

I must have looked confused because she asked, "What did you think the written exam was for? We just wanted to get to know you better!"

At that, I couldn't help but laugh. Ice cream always made everything better.

"Learning to control all your powers will take time," she went on. "But trust me, Mia. You'll learn how to embrace any chaos and mayhem that's bound to come with it."

I nodded, with a big smile across my face.

I *definitely* had a lot to learn . . . but at least I knew I wasn't alone.

"Now, I know it's been an extremely long day, but there's one last step to becoming an official PITS superhero," Dr. Sue Perb said. "A student photo!"

"Okay, Mia. Are you ready? Give me your best superhero pose!" Professor Stu Pendus exclaimed.

After a bunch of different shots, I ran out of ideas. So finally, I just put my hands on my hips.

"Great, Mia! That's the one! Now hold it," Professor Stu Pendus said.

I smiled big and leaned back . . . but turns out, that wasn't the best idea.

"OH NO!" I yelled, reaching my hand out.

Everything instantly froze. Just like at Eddie's house.

Whoa, I still have no idea how I did that. But thank goodness!

I grabbed the light stand and put it back on the floor.

CRASH!

Phew. Okay, before anything else crazy happens, let's recap: I just had the weirdest, most unbelievable week . . . EVER! It was good; it was bad and full of mayhem. But you know what? I'm starting to believe that a little mayhem is okay. Because it turns out all those times I thought I was a total disaster-machine—like when I broke the goalpost or flooded the school hallways—I was actually using my superpowers. I just didn't know it!

And that's why from now on, you can call me Mia Mayhem. I'm the world's newest superhero!

DON'T MISS MIA MAYHEM'S NEXT ADVENTURE!

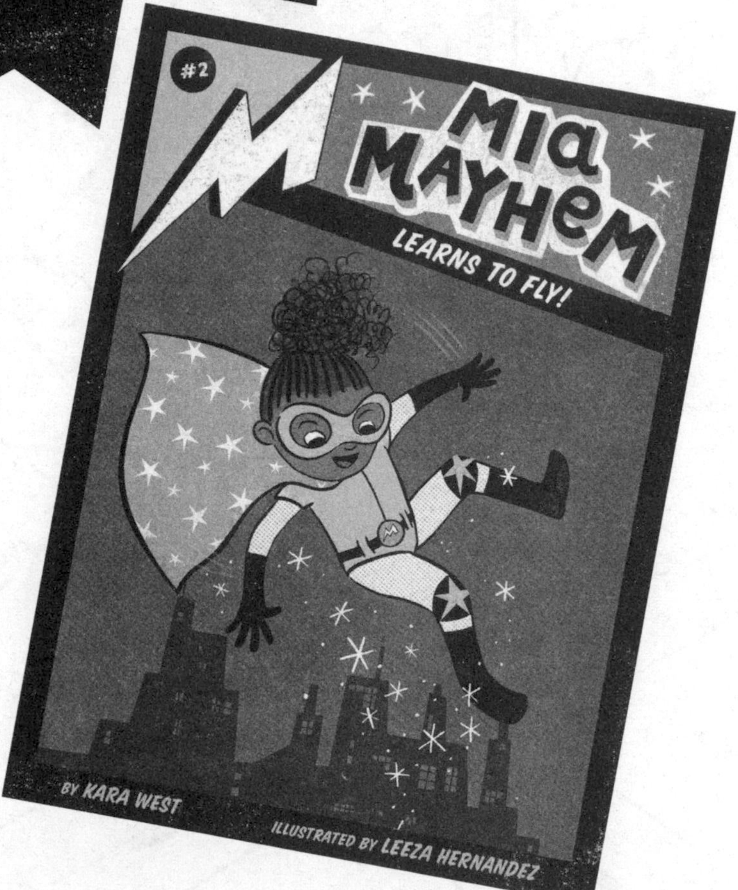